Storm Surge

Archway Publishing books may be ordered through booksellers or by contacting:

Archway Publishing
1663 Liberty Drive
Bloomington, IN 47403
www.archwaypublishing.com
1 (888) 242-5904

ISBN: 978-1-4808-7878-5 (sc)
ISBN: 978-1-4808-7877-8 (e)

Print information available on the last page.

Archway Publishing rev. date: 6/28/2019

Storm Surge

Katie Peterson-Hernandez

Down at the harbor and
just past the dock
a little boat sat
anchored by a rock.

She loved her spot in the shadows of bigger ships, where she could hide from skippers preparing for their trips.

When sailors walked by she'd flap her flags and say, "Oh please don't pick me, today is not my day."

She'd sink her hull
down low, looking small
as she could be,
hiding from the skippers
hoping they wouldn't see.

One day that all changed
as she heard stories
from to and fro.
She thought about it
carefully and decided
she wanted to go.

The little boat had
changed her mind safe
but no longer gleeful.
She left the dock bow pressed
out, looking for some people.

The little boat's heart filled with joy as she dreamed about her day. She prepped her deck and stretched her mast ready to sail away.

The little boat set out to sail
calm and feeling strong.
Then a ripple in the
water told her something
was very wrong.

The storm had rolled in quickly with winds blowing strong and gusty. The little boat curled up her flags fearing they'd get dusty.

A mighty crash filled the air followed by a low and threatening rumble. The little boat was tossed about and her mast began to crumble.

She sucked in her sails
and pressed on forward
with a mighty heave.
As the storm raged on she
dodged the waves with
careful bobs and weaves.

She fought the fearsome
surge feeling it was
all she could take.
Finally the water slowed and
the waves began to break.

The little boat made it to shore safe with the shaken band. She parked her self back at the pier thankful to see land.

As she looked upon the
shore her bow pressed
out with pride.
She was delighted with
what she'd done and
wondered why she'd
ever wanted to hide.

Author Biography

Katie Peterson-Hernandez is a reader, thinker, and mom. She lives in Austin, Texas with her husband, daughters, and a devastatingly handsome English bulldog.

CPSIA information can be obtained
at www.ICGtesting.com
Printed in the USA
BVHW021121131119
R10442900001B/R104429PG563469BVX2B/16/P

9 781480 878785